Bones Of The Sea

AMY LAURENS

OTHER WORKS

SANCTUARY SERIES

Where Shadows Rise
Through Roads Between
When Worlds Collide
The Complete Sanctuary Series

KADITEOS SERIES

How Not To Acquire A Castle

STORM FOXES

A Fox Of Storms And Starlight

SHORTER WORKS

April Showers
Bones Of The Sea
Darkness and Good
Dreaming Of Forests
It All Changes Now
Of Sea Foam and Blood
Rush Job
Trust Issues

INKPRINT WRITERS

How To Write Dogs
How To Theme
How To Create Cultures
How To Create Life
How To Map

Find more works by the author at www.amylaurens.com/books/

BONES OF THE SEA

AMY LAURENS

AUSTRALIA

Print ISBN: 978-1-922434-37-1
eBook ISBN: 9781393738985

www.inkprintpress.com

National Library of Australia Cataloguing-in-Publication Data
Laurens, Amy 1985—
Bones Of The Sea
76 p.   cm.
ISBN: 978-1-922434-37-1
Inkprint Press, Canberra, Australia
1. Fiction—Fantasy—Contemporary 2. Fiction—Fantasy—
Dark Fantasy 3. Fiction—Coming Of Age

Summary: Lucy touches cursed bones to save herself from carnivorous Mist, and now must figure out how to devest herself of the curse before it claims her life.

First Edition: June 2021

Cover design © Inkprint Press.

God, I was too exhausted, too sick, too busy to write this book. Thanks for doing it for me.

Liana, Daimien: thank you both, always.

This book was written on Ngunnawal country, and I acknowledge the people who have told their stories here for countless generations.

BONES OF THE SEA

THE MAN—WHOSE NAME IS IRRELEVANT, FOR HE shall soon be dead—wandered down the beach where sand whiter than any he'd seen before swashed between a short, head-high cliff to his left, and the frothing waves of the ocean to his right. Salt filled the air, but below that, something else lingered, and he couldn't quite place his... nose... on what it was.

Of course, the locals were horrified that he was here at all. But he was a Man Of Learning, and was not accustomed to heeding the warnings of people obviously less learned than himself, especially when they spoke tales of a beach that left no trespasser alive.

He'd scoffed. Ridiculous, their legends of a beach where to set one toe on the sand was to seal your own death sentence before the rising of the next full moon.

He was far more interested in analysing the sand, quite literally whiter than any he'd seen before, and thus far resistant to his attempts to decode it. He'd thought a pure variety of quartz before he'd arrived, but upon reaching the beach, pulling into the little deserted cul-de-sac dead end festooned with warning signs ('Cursed Beach, Do Not Enter'; 'Beware The Bones Of The Sea'), he'd switched his engine off, opened the car door to the sound of waves and wind through the saltbush, and he'd seen the sharp drop-off down to the sand and had changed his mind to chalk, or maybe gypsum.

But there'd been no tiny fossils his portable microscope could detect, and the sand, whatever it was made from, had failed to fizz under the application of a drop of acid from his little glass vial, so that struck gypsum and chalk from the list of options.

Now, after several hours on the beach to no avail as the hot evening sun seared his hands and the light glinting off both ocean and white sand blinded him, he'd had enough. He'd run out of fresh water, ideas, and patience all, and was presently hiking back around the cove to his car that glinted silver and tantalising at the far end of the beach, a haven of cool air and fresh water.

Stay. Stay a little while longer.

The salt clung to his skin, filming his lips, the inside of his nose, the back of his throat. Somehow, the ocean smelled sharper here, more concentrated. Briefly, he wondered if that was the source of the townsfolk's rumours; but a higher salt concentration ought to have meant people floated better, drowned less. No. There must simply be a convergence of factors that meant the currents here were particularly treacherous, and indeed, casting his gaze out to the distant horizon, examining the interplay of wave and off-white foam, the cove did seem to be quite swirly, with a few smooth tracts he thought were probably rips.

As ever, folklore had a logical series of explanations behind it.

Just a little longer.

His leather sandal caught on something in the sand.

He stumbled.

Ow. That hurt.

Whatever it was, it had poked through the holes in his footwear to stab at his toes.

Glaring, impatient, our nameless victim kicked away some of the strange, defiant white sand—and inhaled sharply.

Once the initial burst of adrenalin subsided—something a surprise human skull will inevitably inspire, regardless of one's general composure—it seemed obvious.

Of course. The one thing he hadn't tested for was bone.

So focused on unlocking the mystery of the sand's composition was he that his initial reaction was deep, gleeful satisfaction.

Dawning understanding, however, made him lift his feet, hesitantly at first, shaking the white sand—bone—sand, think of it as sand, it's safer that way—but it's bone, really it's bone, it's all bone, every single grain of it, pure white, sun-bleached bone, spat up from the guts of the ocean the way a predatory owl spits out the bones of its prey—and then his feet were dancing, just like his stomach, as he leapt for the cliff and tried to haul himself up and off the beach because God, oh God, he was standing on bones and only bones, and the skull he'd uncovered had been human, and there, just down the beach, that rock wasn't a rock, it was another skull, and oh God, how many people had died here?

He realised the sobbing was his, rasps of panic as he scrabbled at the embankment that should have been easier to climb than it was, his fingers digging at the rock, skin tearing, sandals scraping for purchase...

Stay.

His back was to the ocean when the freak wave rose, a local tsunami of salt and hunger.

It smashed into him.

As it dragged him out to sea, all he felt was cold, so bitter it froze his bones right in his body.

An hour later, as the sun spilled red-orange lifeblood out over the ocean, the ocean spat a skull, bleached-white and grinning, back up onto the beach. A moment later, as the full moon crested over the craggy headland behind, a sternum—*most* of its ribs still attached—joined the skull, followed a moment later by a single scapula.

And as the moon rose and the ocean swallowed the sun, a whisper began that sounded like the wind... until you realised there was nothing but saltbush for the wind to disturb, and the whispers sounded strangely like a voice, hungry, crooning, and singing.

Feed me.

Feeed mee.

Feeeed meeeeee....

Bones of the forest,
watchful be.
Bones of the meadow,
faithful be.
Bones of the mountains,
truthful be.
But pay no heed
to the bones of the sea.

Due to a fortuitous combination of luck, her mother's well-placed caution, and her own excellent common sense, Lucy had managed to reach the ripe old age of fourteen before seeing the Mist in person.

There'd been that one incident when she was six, of course, when the Mist had curled far from the ocean, all the way through the woods and down into the little valley where they lived, but Mama had done all the right things, turning every air-conditioning unit in the house on full speed, every fan set to whip the chilled air about the rooms, leaving the doors to both fridge and freezer wide open, and packing the whole family into the bathroom, where every tap ran cold water and she thrust herself and Nellie, the three-year-old, under the streaming cold shower, while Lucy sat in a bath where ice cubes floated like icebergs, and the Mist had swept on by with nary an issue.

Lucy could still remember the way her teeth had chattered from the cold and her heart had rattled from the fear, the tears streaming down her cheeks the warmest part of her whole body.

It had been the better part of thirty minutes before their mother, blue-lipped like her daughters, had invited Lucy into the shower and had twisted the tap slowly around to lukewarm, and then warm, and finally hot, before letting them all out to re-dress and making a giant pot of potato and lentil soup.

Dusk had fallen by that time, and the night-screamers were about their evening rituals, scree-ching their haunting cries at the darkening sky.

Unlike the other children at school, Lucy at least had that once experience to cling to, something to anchor the adults' warnings about the Mist, and so she (and Nellie, for although she'd only been three, it had been the kind of experience that had seared itself on the memory) had never been tempted to wander in the direction of the woods, even though she of all of the children lived the closest.

But today.

Today was different.

Fourteen, and full of confidence in her own abilities, Lucy had been sent by her mother to forage for glowing ember fungus for a potion Mama was brewing, and Lucy—fourteen and full of the need to prove herself—had willingly acquiesced, even though just last Tuesday she had bemoaned her mother's apparent need to send her constantly on the most trivial of errands to anyone who'd give an ear to listen.

The difference, perhaps, was that Lucy felt an exploration into the woods to be more important than a trip to the local store for some cultured butter, or a run across the paddocks to the Dossickers' place to urgently borrow a bucket of shale. After all, she'd never dare venture therein before, living as she did with a healthy respect-bordering-on-terror of the Mist.

And so she entered the forest of the Huon pines with adrenalin pumping through her limbs and anticipation fluttering in her stomach, chin held high in defiance both of any lingering trace of fear, and of any who might spontaneously appear to question the legitimacy of her presence here. *She* was fourteen. *She* was responsible—else why would Mama have set her this task?

The scent of the pines closed over her, and she relished the taste in the chill, clean air of another world, another life than the one she'd been previously living. Moss festooned the trunks of the massive pines, trees thousands of years old and tens of feet in diameter, bark deeply creased and folded on some of the oldest, largest trees, and merely rough on those much younger.

It was then that the day began to grow overcast, and indeed, it cast over an edge on Lucy's mood, a slight sense of foreboding or subtle misgiving about her adventure.

She quickened her pace, scrambling over leaf litter dropped last autumn from the tanglefoot trees—barely twice her height, with roots and branches equally thin and gnarled—hopping over fallen branches, and at last crunching her way across the gravelly bed of a barely running stream.

The stream was a good sign; on the map Mama had drawn for her, the most promising area for glowing embers was marked just a little way beyond.

And that was when Lucy heard the unmistakeable sound of other footfalls close by in the forest.

She froze, self-conscious and exposed on a smooth, round boulder the size of her head in the middle of the stream bed, heart racing, throat suddenly dry.

Goosebumps rose on her arms, prickling at her skin and making her suddenly aware of how the temperature had dropped; she hadn't noticed it while warm from the exertion of walking.

The bushes in front of her rustled.

She tensed even further.

A pademelon, small, brown and really rather adorable in any other circumstance, burst out of the bushes into the stream bed, hop-hoppitying away as fast as its little kangaroo legs could carry it.

Lucy snorted at herself, gave her biceps a brisk rub—and froze again as the sound of footsteps resumed, this time at pace.

A monster? A madman? A warlock come to assault her and steal her away? Her mind was alive with the terrifying possibilities, such that when a blond boy about her own age burst into the stream bed and screeched to a red-faced halt, it took her a moment to find her tongue. "What... What are you doing here?"

It was Edgar, someone she almost called a friend at school (and possibly would have called a friend had he not been so confoundedly good looking), and he was wide-eyed, red-cheeked, and panting.

High up in the branches of an ancient pine, a nightscreamer screamed.

"Run," Edgar gasped. He reached out his hand for her.

The flutter in her chest at the thought of touching his hand held her attention momentarily.

He gestured impatiently. *"Mist,"* he said. *"Run."*

Right. Mist. Run.

Lucy whirled, snatched up his hand, and tried her best not to fall as they pelted through the forest, where the air had suddenly gone chill, the light draining away like something was devouring it.

Her side grabbed; a stitch.

The saliva in her throat was thick, choking.

And behind them, the Mist crept forward inexorably, not so much white as silver, luminescent, obscuring sun and sky so completely that it felt like moonlight on a deep, shining night.

"Not… going to make it," Lucy panted out, her free hand clutching the wicker basket she'd brought for the fungus so tightly her hand hurt. She was gripping Edgar's hand even more tightly, but as he was gripping hers tightly back, that seemed only fair.

He jerked her along for a few more steps, her shoulder screaming, her lungs protesting, the fear not quite enough to override her body's sheer inability to run any faster, or any farther at this frenetic pace.

Edgar stopped.

Lucy wasn't the only one who leaned over, gasping for air.

"Bones," he spat out, and for a moment Lucy thought it was a peculiar kind of swear word.

Then she realised what he meant, and her stomach did a complicated little twist; she knew enough from listening at the fringes of Mama's conversations for fourteen years to wish it had just been a swear word.

"We can't touch *bones*," she hissed, eyes round, wide. She held the basket up in front of her like a shield.

It was a rule as cast in iron as the ones about avoiding the Mist; around here, you Didn't Touch Bones.

Not fish bones when you fished for them in the ocean to the east (never the west, avoid the western ocean at any and every cost), not deer bones when you hunted them, not cow bones when you slaughtered them, not chicken bones when you butchered them, not any bones, not here, not ever. It was complicated, at times, and somewhat convoluted, but even the tiny emergency hospital sent people north to have anything to do with bones mended.

Lucy wasn't *quite* sure what would happen if you touched a bone, but the precautions everyone took to avoid them had ingrained upon her the direst sense of urgency about that one thing, if nothing else, ever:

One Did Not Touch Bones.

Cousin Tommy had, that once when they were eight. Lucy's aunt had taken him away and spanked him, and when he'd finally been allowed to play with them again weeks later, he'd refused to talk about the incident—and had refused even more vociferously to have anything to do with bones, ever again.

But... that wasn't the unabridged story.

Because, like any cursed subject, bones were a prominent feature in child's play round about here, and everyone knew the rhymes.

Bones of the forest, watchful be.

It meant watchful in the same way as 'watch out' did; to keep watch, to warn—to protect.

Lucy's throat was burning, too dry, too clogged.

Edgar's face practically glowed red in the eerie light.

The Mist was a scant hundred paces or so behind, drifting ghost-like through the trees.

They'd been running, and they were both over-heated, and normal body temperature was bad enough let alone when you were practically radiating heat like this for the Mist to find you, and they had no other way of cooling themselves down fast enough, or even just *enough*, and the meadow was too far away, and besides, if the Mist had come this far then what was to stop it reaching all the way up the valley to the house today, like it had that one time years ago, and there was no human way they could outrun the Mist all the way back to house, and they were going to die.

The Mist was going to devour them, and they were going to die.

Tommy didn't die when he touched the bones.

Bones of the forest, watchful be.

It wasn't logical, but it was a chance where none other was to be had.

"Bones," Lucy said, nodding with what she hoped was decisiveness and not panic. Certainly that little squeak in her voice was a hangover from her exertion, and not the timbre of fear.

Edgar flailed again for her hand. "I saw some," he said. "On my way in. Close." He pointed upward and ahead of them, and for a confused moment Lucy wondered that she might see bones hanging in a tree—but no, he was pointing to King Jack, the tallest and most ancient of the Huon pines, a landmark in a forest of similar-looking trees festooned with similar-looking moss.

They jogged, casting nervous glances back over their shoulders at the Mist—still ghosting toward them, swallowing tree trunks one by one—then skirted around King Jack's massive girth.

"Somewhere near here," Edgar said, motioning her to spread out and hunt.

Lucy did, footfalls somewhere between a rustle and a squelch in the damp leaf litter, trying hard to ignore the way the tip of her nose was growing cold, the ridges of her cheeks, her forehead, the tip of her chin.

She'd worn long sleeves, but her shirt was thin, soaked now from sweat that she could smell when she tilted her chin down to survey the ground, and her teeth were beginning to think about chattering.

Bones.

Bones.

It was a forest, surely there had to be bones.

A cry from Edgar not four feet to her left drew her attention. She whipped around, saw the partial skull with a stub of an antler, joined Edgar in crouching by its side.

Mould or mildew or some sort of moss greened the crevices of the skull. It looked like it belonged on Mother's shelf of oddities, the ingredients she kept in reserve for the trickiest of her workings.

"On three?"

Lucy glanced over at Edgar's honey-brown eyes—at the Mist curling behind him. She nodded, praying to anything that might be listening that this would work.

Death by Mist was *not* something she wanted to investigate.

"One."

Lucy reached out and clutched Edgar's hand.

"Two."

She inhaled sharply, pine and decaying leaves and something frozen, metallic and salty filling her senses.

"Three."

They touched the skull at the same time.

Lucy had no way of knowing what Edgar was experiencing, but *her* world exploded suddenly into vibrant, golden light, a heart of deepest purple some indeterminate distance away in front of her, the feeling of warm showers massaging down on her back, a wetness that was dry, a warmth that was cool, suffused with the sensation of deep, ancient, vast, immeasurable *knowing*.

She had just enough wits left to realise that this was an experience she could never recover from; forever after, everything in her life would be compared to this one, single, perfect instant of clarity and belonging, where she was one with the universe and it was one with her.

And then the deep purple heart in all the golden light resolved, and it was an eye, watchful, and purposeful—and furious.

Lucy screamed.

Heat blasted from the golden eye with its huge, horizontal-oval pupil.

She ducked. No, she *cowered*.

But the heat washed over her, tingling her body from head to toe like the deepest, purest sensation imaginable—and behind her, a sharp metallic *clang* as the light collided with… something.

She turned, still crouching.

A wall of silver and gold, a blaze of light…

And then nothing.

Nothing, except the feel of Edgar's hand in hers, warm, and solid, and human.

Thrice for thee
And thrice for me
And thrice again
For the bones of the sea.

For an indeterminately long time, they lay in darkness together, with thoughts so fractured and spiralling that there were no words to share between them, only the warm, steady pressure of each other's hands anchoring them together there in infinity.

Eventually, they were released back to the forest, and found themselves lying, cold and wet and shivering, on the ground near the partial skull, old King Jack standing watch nearby as dusk thickened into twilight.

Insects chirruped and clicked in the trees, night-screamers screamed their haunted cries back and forth to each other like the possessed little demon birds they were, and somewhere in the middle distance, a wallaby sneezed.

Carefully, as though given bodies suddenly made of glass, Edgar and Lucy pulled themselves to their feet and tried to brush off their clothing.

Edgar's lips twisted as he watched Lucy contort, stretching to brush the dirt and leaf matter from her back. "Here," he said. "Let me." Gently, he removed the worst of the forest from her shirt, then turned around so she could do the same for him.

In virtual silence, the pair made their way from the damp-scented forest, stopping only once to gather up a handful of glowing ember fungus that hung on the side of a single middle-aged pine, the light of the fungus already beginning to cast a bluish glow over its immediate surrounds as the last line of sea green licked the western sky.

The air in the meadows seemed sweeter, warmer, and as though they'd held a rational discussion and mutually agreed upon it, they let go of each other's hands.

Just as easily, they parted ways when Lucy reached the beginnings of the little track that wound up toward the back of her house, Edgar continuing on through the knee-high grasses, some with prickly seed heads already, most with the feathery tuffs that passed for flowers when you were a grass, releasing their bitter pollen into the night air.

After all, it wasn't as though there'd been some grand gesture tying them together. They'd shared an experience, but as a pair of individuals. Not as anything else.

Above, stars twinkled.

Lucy breathed deeply as she set foot on her back porch, steeling herself for whatever might lie ahead. No doubt her mother would be frantic at her prolonged absence. Would the welcome be coloured by relief, or fear and punishment?

Only one way to find out.

Lucy grasped the iron knob, and opened the door with the tortuous creak that was her mother's idea of a burglar alarm.

A chair scraped the kitchen floor: Mama, standing abruptly and starting toward Lucy, leaving a steaming mug of something calming on the table.

But Mama stopped midway, Lucy still in the liminal zone of the doorway, neither in the house nor out, and Mama stared, crestfallen, mouth dropping softly open before she reached up to press her fingertips against her lips as tears sprang to her eyes.

"Mama," Lucy said, closing the door behind her (another tortured screech). "Mama, I'm okay. I'm back, I'm okay." She dropped the fungus basket on the floor.

Her mother shook her head, scooped Lucy into her arms, all warmth and sap-smell and sweetness. "You've been bone cursed," she whispered into Lucy's dark hair, gripping Lucy in a hug so tight it felt like one of them might drown. "Oh, Lucy, I should never have sent you. I'm sorry. I'm so, so sorry."

The chill ran not down Lucy's back, as chills were wont to do, but rather through the actual bones of her spine, as though something had latched its icy fingers into them and was tugging experimentally to see how strong its grasp might be. "But they let me go, Mama. The bones saved us from the Mist, and they let us go." She was crying, and she wasn't quite sure which part of the ordeal was responsible.

And in the back of her mind, still the golden light flared, vast and immeasurable and knowing.

"No, my love," her mama said, thumbing the tears from Lucy's cheek. "The bones never let you go."

Lucy stared up into clear, brown eyes. "Did I do the wrong thing?" she whispered. *Should I have let the Mist take me?*

She shuddered as images sprang to mind unbidden, the picked-clean carcasses of sheep and cattle who'd strayed too close to the Mist when it was over-hungry; the fields of their neighbours eight years ago that had looked like cattle boneyards. It had taken months to move all those bleached, stark bones safely from the fields.

"Oh, sweetheart." Mama crushed her again in a hug so encompassing it almost vanquished the lingering golden light. "You did the only thing you could. But now..." She pushed Lucy back to arm's length, scrutinised her face. "We will have to pay the price."

Bones, it turned out, were slow to collect their debts.

A year was nearly long enough for the crest-fallen micro-expression on Mama's face to ebb from a minutely occurrence, every time she saw Lucy, to merely a weekly one.

Lucy welcomed the change, welcomed the moments when she too could forget…

And then cousin Tommy died.

Well, missing presumed dead, last seen walking in the direction of the western ocean.

There was no body found—but then, there never were bodies to be found in that direction. Bone fragments and partial skeletons were all the cruel sea ever offered them back, and every one of them in the area knew better than to set foot on the beach in some vain attempt to reclaim the remains of the once-living.

Tommy had just turned fifteen. He'd been eight when he touched the bones, so Lucy figured she had six years left to figure out how exactly the curse worked, and what exactly she could do to avoid its nasty ending.

"Mama," she said, entering the kitchen, the slate floor cold against her bare feet, one of Mama's potions lingering sweet and complex in the air, brushing against her cheek as a cat might against her ankles. "Who knows most about the curse?"

Mama set aside the wooden spoon she was using to stir the grey-green contents of a saucepan on the stove, turned down the heat so the potion would simmer gently unsupervised, and sat at the three-person table near the remains of the old open hearth.

It was an old house. The table looked like it belonged.

Lucy sat opposite, the inside of her lower lip between her teeth, eyebrows knit together under her mother's intense scrutiny.

"Here's what I've learned," Mama began briskly, and Lucy's eyebrows had the naive audacity to drift upwards a little.

Of *course* Mama had been researching the curse. Of course she had.

Lucy had too, but she'd found her enquiries to be of relatively limited use: her only contacts were either children and thus as ignorant as herself, or adults and thus disinclined to converse on the subject with her. Edgar and she had made many a speculation together, of course, but it was no substitute for actual, concrete knowledge, and the lack of it weighed in her stomach like a knot of cold fear.

"One, there's no escaping it." Mama ticked the item off on her forefinger. "People have tried to run and people have tried to hide, and as far as living memory is aware, there isn't anybody who's managed to outrun the bones yet.

"Two." Her middle finger joined the forefinger. "Seven seems to be important, and so do three and nine. People are always taken by the bones after three or seven or nine years, and no one seems to have developed a functional theory about who gets three years to get their affairs in order and who gets nine."

Lucy's stomach swirled. "Three? I thought it was always seven!"

Tommy had had seven years. And Macy at school, the only non-adult who knew personally someone else who'd been cursed, said that her uncle had had seven years as well, now that she thought on it.

Lucy might only have two more years to live.

Her throat knotted. She clenched her jaw and swiped angrily at the tears that prickled her eyes.

Mama reached over and took Lucy's hand, her own hand warm and calloused from her work. She waited for Lucy's gaze to find her, then stared unflinchingly with her clear, brown eyes. "You will have only three. I can feel it."

Something inside Lucy snapped. One moment she was sitting at the table, and the next she was slumped over it, unable to hold herself up, unable to stop the silent tears flowing, unable to think past the number pounding over and over with her heartbeat: One, two. One, two. One, two.

She was going to die at the age of seventeen, and there was nothing that could be done to stop it.

"Stop that," Mama said sharply. "Of course there is something to be done."

Two years. What could she do with only two more years? She'd wanted to travel, she'd wanted to—

Lucy blinked.

Her mind caught up with her ears.

She sat up. "What do you mean?"

Mama smiled, and it was sad and crooked—but it was still a smile. "I didn't finish my list." She wriggled the two fingers she'd counted on.

Slowly, Lucy nodded. Mucous was clogging her nose. She cast about for a tissue or a handkerchief before gratefully accepting a square of paper towel from Mama.

She blew her nose, coughed, and—inhaling a deep breath of the steam from the sweet, fruity green potion wafting off the stove—sat straight again. "Okay," she said. "I'm okay." She nodded as if agreeing with her own words would lend them further credulity.

Mama nodded back, accepting the charade. "Three." A third finger joined the first two. "You know I learned much of what I know from Granny Wetherwack when I was a girl."

Lucy nodded, this time meaningfully.

"She left me her books when she died. I've been combing through them the last twelve months, hoping to find something useful."

Lucy's pulse quickened. Granny Wetherwack's library had been legendary: not the usual kind of books one found at school, or in a bookstore, or even in a library, no. These books were mostly handwritten, mostly full of recipes and garden journals and notes about the livestock Granny had tended— but full of the most intriguing marginalia Lucy had ever seen. Strange potions with unrecognised ingredients, ditties and skipping rhymes three centuries out of date, spidery sketches of plants and animals sometimes as common as wheat and cows, and sometimes as strange as oddly jointed creatures rising out of otherwise flat, clear water. "What did you find?" she asked.

Mama pursed her lips. "Many things," she said. "None particularly clear."

That had always been the way of it. Granny had died when Mama was only twelve, and although she'd taught Mama a great deal more than any other twelve-year-old knew before she passed, nevertheless she'd barely managed to put a dent in the seemingly insurmountable trove of knowledge that she had to impart—and deciphering the rest from the library was the work of a lifetime.

Abruptly, Mama rose, wooden chair scraping on the floor. She turned to the stove, lifting the lid on the saucepan. A cloud of steam rose, billowing out and thickening the air with sweet liquorice and wolfberry.

Lucy waited patiently.

(There was nothing else to be done when Mama was focusing on one of her potions. Mama would return in a moment, and the conversation would continue, and the potion would continue as all the others had: largely backdrop to Lucy's life, an ever-changing but ever-constant presence as Mama brewed and stirred and healed and gave life.)

Only, this time, Mama lifted the spoon to sniff at the translucent grey-green liquid, inhaling deeply. "It's ready," she said. The spoon clinked twice on the side of the pan, then Mama was pouring the liquid out into a tall double-walled glass and delivering it to Lucy.

It wasn't that Lucy wasn't used to drinking her mother's concoctions; that was a daily affair.

But it had been a very long time, maybe five or six years, since Mama had given her one to drink that she didn't immediately recognise.

"What is it?" Lucy lifted the tall glass and inhaled as Mama had done. The scent was delicious, sweet but not overbearing, gently aniseed, a distant trace of mint. She had it in her hands and pressing against her lips without even waiting for Mama to answer.

"It *should*," Mama said slowly, eyes fixed to the potion as Lucy downed it, "allow you to touch the bones again without cost."

Lucy's eyes went wide and she coughed as the last mouthful of the potion hit the back of her throat, sweet and hot and sharp. "*What?*"

Across the table, Mama's eyes glistened.

Outside, a nightscreamer shrieked—and Lucy glanced out the window, surprised to see dusk gilding the western sky.

"I think," Mama said, still using that same careful, measured tone, "that it may even help. May give us some answers. But first..." She met Lucy's gaze.

"First it should let you safely touch the bones."

Lucy's mouth froze, unable to choose which words to form first.

How did you find this?

Were the ingredients costly?

If it will let me touch the bones, why didn't Granny make this for everyone in the whole district?

Why didn't Granny save people?

"I know," Mama said softly. "I know. And I don't know. Maybe it doesn't work. Maybe it only works if you've already touched the bones once. I don't know." She buried her face in her hands. "It was the only thing I could find. It might not even work."

Slowly, Lucy's tongue unfroze—and then the rest of her, one tiny, minute untightening at a time. She stretched across the table and put her hand on Mama's head, fingers deep in Mama's thick, dark hair. "Thank you," she whispered. "For trying."

Lucy's chair scraped back.

"Where are you going?" Mama's look was sharp, hooded in fear and worry.

"To try," Lucy said simply. It was the least she could do, and there was a cow carcass out there in the close paddock, meat mostly stripped, hip bones plainly visible through a tear in its hide, that the cleanup crew hadn't showed up to remove yet.

After all. What was the worst that could happen?

The sweet liquorice of the potion still lingering in the back of her mouth, Lucy stepped out into the dusk and crossed the grass, climbed through the wire fence—and stood over the carcass of the jersey cow, heart suddenly pounding fit to burst.

Mama stood at her shoulder, squeezed her once, twice, for comfort—Mama's or Lucy's, she couldn't say.

Lucy crouched.

Her heart pounded harder.

Was it only a moment ago that she'd finished the potion? Her mouth felt dry, dry as a... well, a bone.

Lucy worked moisture back into her mouth, still cold from the mint and aniseed, even though the potion had been warm.

Above, the first stars began glimmering into sight.

Lucy chewed her lip.

Stretched out her hand.

The carcass of the cow stank sweetly of rotting meat and decay. The grass around it already grew thick and lush, cool in the twilight, dark as the sun left the sky.

Closer.

She forgot how to breathe.

Would these bones draw her in like the stag had, send her spinning and reeling into some over-bearingly bright, chaotic world?

Only one way to know.

Her fingers met bone, and a small part of her was relieved to discover that the bone was indeed dry;

that small part had been convinced the bone would feel slimy, surrounded as it was by rot.

She just had time to slump a little with that small, specific relief—and a pulse of darkness burst forth from the carcass of the cow, knocking her back.

Lucy fell in a tangle of limbs, half flung across her mother as a bolt of darkness shot up into the nearly night-time sky. Far above, it flared, bursting into coruscating light like falling stars...

And when Lucy blinked the afterglow from her eyes, she realised that, on the grass in front of her, right at her feet, was a murky shape also of limbs and bright eyes like stars...

A fox, or at least, a fox-like creature, made equally of bones and shadow.

Her breath caught in her throat as the scent of minerals curled around her. "What is it?" she whispered.

Her mother squeezed her arm and extricated herself so she could stand. "I don't know."

Lucy swallowed. The creature, about the size of a beagle, might have been drawn by the potion... or it might not have. It might harm her... or it might help her.

Only one way to know.

She stretched out her hand again, tentative, hesitant, offering the back of her hand to the darkness-and-bones in vulpine form, and waited for it to bite— or sniff.

Instead, she squeaked in surprise as the creature licked the back of her hand—did foxes do that, usually??—and whirled away, dancing a few steps to the wire-strung fence before whirling back and dancing in place, star-eyes fixed, it seemed, on Lucy.

"I think…"

"Yes," her mother said, for there was really little doubt to be had that the creature wanted Lucy to follow it.

Lucy set her jaw and clambered to her feet. The potion really had chilled her mouth; the inside of her cheeks felt cold, and dry.

The fox yipped impatiently.

"Can you come with me, do you think?" Lucy asked Mama, eyeing the creature of bones.

Mama stepped forward, following Lucy as she in turn followed the skeletal fox.

The fox bared its teeth, darkness curling back like jowls from gleaming white points. Its star eyes narrowed.

Fear chilled through Lucy's chest.

"I think not," Mama replied.

Lucy nodded, less agreement—though it wasn't *not* agreement—than resolution. What must be done must be done, and if she had to do it alone… Well. Mama was hardly going to pave the way when it was time for the curse to take her, after all, so she might as well get used to doing things alone.

But as she stepped away, preparing to duck through the wire fence after the little creature who was, even now, dancing fitfully across the meadow in fits and starts, Mama grabbed her from behind, both hands on her shoulders, and drew her close.

Lucy closed her eyes, Mama's warmth enclosing her from behind.

"I love you," Mama said.

"I love you too."

The fox yipped.

Lucy squeezed Mama's hand, once, very tight, then broke away to follow the fox's dancing, jittery steps through long grasses whose seed heads tickled at her elbows.

It was cold.

She should have brought long sleeves.

At the edge of the forest, a chill shuddered through her that, while initiated by the cold, had rather more of the darkness in it than the temperature.

It wasn't that she hadn't been to the woods since that fateful day a little over a year ago.

It wasn't even that she hadn't been to the woods in the dark; glowing ember fungus was much easier to spot in dim lighting, and even now she could see a cluster of it under the fork of one of the tanglefoot trees, a few paces in on her right.

But something about tonight, *this* night, brought goosebumps to her arms and a certain stuttering to her pulse.

A puff of breath coalesced in front of her.

That stilled her completely.

Only the Mist was that visible at night time. And it was night time now indeed, full dark, with a heavy-handed smatter of stars swathed above her and only the faintest rim of green liming the western horizon, barely visible ahead through the trees, and she shouldn't have been able to see her breath.

Unless the Mist was up.

The fox came back, circling around her and nipping at her ankles when she wouldn't move.

It all came down to the potion. To trust.

Did she trust her mother? Did she trust Granny, and the information in those ancient, crumbling journals?

Lucy sniffed. Of course she did.

Ouch. She jerked her foot aside.

She trusted her mother, and the fox's nipping was becoming quite insistent. So, fine then: she entered the woods at night with the shimmer of Mist in the air and the scent of the sea drifting in on the occasional breeze.

After all, what could the Mist do that she hadn't already been condemned to?

Lucy ground her teeth and marched on, leaf litter shushing her footsteps, fingernails biting her palms.

Behind her, the moon drifted lazily into the sky, a full orb shining with reflected light that filtered down through the thick canopy, shifting and striating and throwing the woods into unearthly shadow and light.

Several times, her heart jumping in her chest, Lucy though she caught sight of someone walking toward her through the night; beings tall, and thin, and grasping...

But every time she blinked, and stared a little harder, and nothing was there, and all was still well—or at least as well as it could be when you were cursed to death from touching bones, which you'd only done because the Mist rolling in off the sea wanted to devour you then and there, and it had all come down to a choice between inevitable death now, or inevitable death later.

Strangely, the thought made Lucy brighten. Her shoulders relaxed a little and she lifted her chin; fated to die, it seemed, damned if she did and damned if she didn't—and the glorious thing about that was that it meant none of it had been her own fault. For months now she'd held the seed festering in her heart, the black suspicion that perhaps, if only, she ought to have done something different on that fateful first day in the forest.

But now, as she followed the skeleton fox, its bones woven together with darkness and shadow, its footsteps inaudible in the quiet night, she realised that she'd been doomed to die regardless, and that perhaps it wasn't so evil, so selfish of her to have chosen the prolonged death rather than the instant one.

A nightscreamer shrieked—but Lucy still smiled.

They reached the far side of the woods, however, and the smile was jolted off her face. The moon stood a handspan above the horizon behind her now, high enough that it was peeking over the tops of the tallest Huon pines, gleaming and glimmering in its field studded with stars.

In front of her, an abandoned road separated the woods from the sea—and Lucy's breath caught in her throat, because there, rolling out before her endless and ever onward, was the ocean. The salty scent wound through her breaths, her thoughts; the cold breeze kicking up against her face made her acutely aware of the tip of her nose, of the tops of her cheekbones, of the point of her chin.

She fought the urge to lick her lips.

The fox whined.

Lucy glanced down, surprised to see it so close— she'd forgotten it for just a second, there, with the rolling expanse of the sea in front of her, the waves shifting and tossing, restless in glittering moonlight.

The fox nipped her ankles again.

And abruptly, Lucy realised she could hear more than the shushing of the ocean, waves gushing in and out, in and out, in and out.

And that shadow, there, climbing down the embankment from the road, nearly to the sand—her heart jolted, adrenalin squeezed through her like ice. That *was* a person.

The fox leapt into a run, dashing toward the embankment.

Lucy followed.

And as she neared the other person, adrenalin speared her again: it wasn't a stranger, it was Edgar.

"Edgar!" she screamed. "Stop, no!"

It was only lucky he was moving so slowly, drifting like the moon, like the Mist, as though in a trance.

Lucy threw herself off the embankment, stumbling as she hit the sand, threw herself forward again and snatched at his arm. She whirled him around to face her.

He stared, a little blank, a little glazed, a little awed.

"Edgar." Her voice caught, but it didn't matter. "Edgar it's me, it's Lucy. What are you doing here? You have to go home. We have to get you home." She tugged gently at his arm, but he stood immovable and untouchable as a carcass of bones.

The fox yipped quietly, dancing back and forth but always between Edgar and the ocean.

The tide ran in.

Lucy stared in horror at the encroaching water, silver and black, bones and shadow. She lacked a wealth of experience when it came to large bodies of water, but she was relatively certain that tides didn't usually turn quite *this* fast.

She stepped back, dragging Edgar with her.

A second step.

A third, across the fine, pale sand of the beach, fingers clutching at Edgar's shirt.

The fox bared its teeth and snarled at the water.

"Edgar." Lucy's voice was hoarse. She licked her lips. Salt. "Edgar, we have to go."

He stood as though taking root, staring at the incoming sea.

The cold rock and packed dirt of the embankment pressed against Lucy's back. She could scramble back up, probably, if she used the old tree root sticking out over her shoulder, if she jumped, if she was lucky.

She couldn't get Edgar up though, not without him helping.

The fox snarled again and snapped its teeth.

The sound was oddly loud in the night-time quiet, and Lucy realised the waves had all but fallen silent; instead of breaking, the swell was surging, running up the beach toward her, closer, closer…

The water lapped at her shoes.

Her chest was tight. Adrenalin lit her veins on fire.

The rock behind her was cold, so cold, and the water was coming in, seeping through the fabric of her shoes, trickling down into them, lapping around her ankles.

"Please Edgar, please." She tugged at his arm, knowing it was futile.

Abruptly the fox whirled to stare at her, star-gaze boring into Lucy's. It was either trying to communicate something, or else it was assessing her, as deeply as she'd ever been scrutinised in her life.

It danced backward a few steps, deeper into the water. Inviting her in.

Lucy's heart pounded. Sweat slicked her neck, chilling instantly in the night air.

Bones.

The bones had tried to save her from the Mist.

And maybe—maybe—if the ocean took her, it wouldn't need Edgar as well.

She could still taste the last, lingering remains of Mama's potion, cold and sweet like love, the taste heightened by the contrast with the chill, salty breeze.

Lucy inhaled deeply. "Stay here," she murmured to Edgar, not even sure if he was sensible enough to hear her right now or not.

She bent down. Scooped up the fox. Blinked when she realised it was soft and warm, despite its cold, bony appearance.

The fox complied willingly.

And so, arms full of her bony guide, back to the friend she was trying to save, heart pounding like she'd run the whole way here, Lucy stepped forward, deeper into the water.

Knees.

Oh, the water was cold. So cold.

Thighs.

Like ice.

She winced as her hips went under.

Cold.

Cold, cold, cold.

She couldn't hold the fox above the water any longer. Its tail drooped into the sea. Lucy hugged it to her tightly as her waist submerged, and then the awful, freezing, breath-stealing moment as her chest went under as well.

Neck deep was better. At least the submerged part of her was warmer now.

She looked back. Edgar was still there, pressed against the embankment, the moon rising over his head behind the woods.

Lucy's lips quirked, just a little, one side only, not a smile, because it wasn't happy, but satisfaction perhaps, or maybe relief. The water had stopped rising. It seemed the ocean wanted only one victim tonight after all.

The fox snuggled against her, tucking its muzzle—warm despite all logical assumptions—up behind Lucy's ear.

She cradled it between head and shoulder, and almost without meaning to, began to idly stroke the back of its head and hum.

A little bird sat in a cherry tree
singing the songs of the bones to me.

It was a song her mother had sung to her when she'd been little; a song she remembered almost as much from hearing Mama sing it to Nellie in the next room as she did from Mama singing it to her.

But as it ever had, the song brought a pleasant warmth to her memories, a certain softness to her thoughts, and Lucy smiled as she thought of home.

The fox licked her ear.

Lucy giggled. After all, why not? The ocean had ceased its swelling, had grown calm and flat and quiet. The moon was rising higher, silvering the world, and all was still. Cocooned like this in the ocean, Lucy almost felt warm.

She glanced back at Edgar, still stuporous against the bank, then at the water covering her shoulders. Surely... This was not what she'd been led to believe. Not the climax of decades—maybe centuries—of stories warning her away from the ocean, warning her away from the bones. Not the culmination of a curse that had led so many loved ones to their deaths.

And after all, Edgar had been about to become one of them: stuporous as he was, she doubted he'd have done much more than walk straight on out into the water until he breathed it in.

Was that the key, then? That she'd come early? That she'd come willingly? That she'd come before the stupor had set in?

Surely it was too complicated for that. Someone else would have tried that before now. Surely.

She cast her mind back to Mama and her potion, seeing in her mind's eye images of Mama hunched over and reading furiously, that little frown on her face as she puzzled out the meanings in Granny's journals.

In the stillness of the night, the water surged.

A wave snatched Lucy down.

She screamed—or tried to.

Water filled her mouth. Burned her nose.

She coughed, but underwater there was nothing to replace the ocean in her mouth but more ocean.

The fox scrabbled against her, and for one heart-wrenching moment Lucy thought it was trying to escape, and she couldn't blame it at all—

But then she realised it was trying to swim, trying to *follow* her as she drifted down, and down, and down.

Lucy grabbed at the fox, desperate for anything that might help as the ocean current dragged her away from the shore.

Sand bumped her roughly from below, once, twice—and then a sense of darkness, stillness, pressure, *depth*—and Lucy knew the bottom was far too far away to bump her now. Her ears hurt from the pressure; her sinuses popped like her head was going to explode.

Something bumped her from behind.

Frantic, Lucy whirled in water dark as night. Was she more afraid of what she might see, or what she might *not* see?

The ghostly, glowing shape shocked her so utterly that she gasped, forgetting the water that surrounded her.

Saline gushed inward—

And she breathed.

Perfectly fine.

Lucy's eyes widened and for an instant her shock at that was great enough to displace the shock of the great whale skeleton before her. She could breathe. She was underwater, ocean only knew how deep… and she could breathe.

The sinus pain dissipated.

She inhaled deeply, a long draught that filled her right, so it felt, to her toes.

The whale skeleton nudged her again, and for a moment it seemed clouded in darkness like the fox was clouded, an orca made of shadow and bone.

The fox.

Lucy started, peering around. But the fox was still there, drifting calmly over her right shoulder. She reached out and gently took hold of it; it nuzzled happily against her. Briefly, she thought of home, of snuggling against Mama's shoulder when she said goodnight at bedtime.

Did something glitter briefly in the darkness?

A seahorse skeleton floated past, chasing the glittering sparkles.

Lucy tracked it as it meandered away—then wondered how she could see it in darkness so absolute that even her own body was nothing more than a suggestion in the water below her eyes.

But perhaps it didn't do to dwell on questions such as those when she was also breathing underwater. Much better to close her eyes and remember Nellie giggling, to concentrate on the herbal smell of the kitchen, the sound of one of Mama's potions bubbling away on the stove; much kinder to remember Edgar's shy smile, Mama's cool, calm eyes, the dusty smell of Granny's old journals.

(There must be phosphorescence down here; another tiny trail of sparkles drifted past.)

The whale nudged her a third time, less gentle now, trying to nip at her with its large, pointy teeth. She winced. Those she could see all too well in the gloom.

The fox snarled at the whale, silent as the current pressing down on Lucy's eardrums.

Absently, she soothed it, stroking its head and ears.

Mm. The potion. It had summoned the fox, apparently, and Lucy had thought that was the end of it. But what if it had summoned the orca whales too?

But now what? Surely this wasn't how all the others had ended, breathing underwater and perfectly alive. So what would happen? Would this strange ability wear off, and that was how she'd end?

"What do I do now?" she asked, not really meaning to, and blinked as bubbles left her mouth. Her lungs were full of seawater… weren't they? So where had the air for the bubbles come from?

But that wasn't half so puzzling as what happened next: a second orca joined the first, emerging from the depths like a submarine, huge and ghostly-glimmering, setting Lucy's pulse racing.

Come, the answer came, from the orcas, from the ocean, from all around. *Come with us now. Come home.*

Lucy shook her head. "I have a home. It isn't here." That called up another memory, one of her bedroom, snug and warm and safe, smelling of sage and lavender and love in much the same way as the protective potion her mother had given her also tasted of love.

This time, the glittering was very definitely around her fingers. Lucy lifted her hand in front of her face and stared at it. Phosphorescence? Surely not, not just around her fingers like that, not at this depth.

Memories, someone said, and as it was the fox who turned toward her as the voice came, Lucy assumed that that was who had spoken.

A tiny fish darted in from the darkness of the sea and nibbled at the sparks.

"Oy, hey, *hey*! Those are *my* memories," Lucy said, snatching her hand back.

Our memories now, the whales said—or was it the ocean who said it? Lucy couldn't have said for sure, and the longer she stared at the whales, the more she wondered if perhaps there wasn't any difference between them and the ocean anyway. She made a fist around the now-faded sparkles of her memories. *This is what we have longed for,* the whales continued. *What we have sought for so long.*

A sense of time and distance and age hit Lucy square in the chest, so profound that had she not already been surrounded by salt water, her eyes would have contributed some to wash her face.

She rubbed a hand over her cheeks anyway, hugging the fox tight with her other arm. "But surely the others had memories, too," she said. Memories were what the ocean wanted? That hardly made any sense.

But, *No,* said the ocean via the orcas. *Not these memories.*

Lucy's brow wrinkled.

Family, said the fox, and understanding clicked into place.

It hadn't been any old memories the orcas had been attracted too—or the seahorse, or the fish, come to think of it. It had been the specific, precise memories of her family.

Narrowing her eyes, Lucy tried to call to mind the taste of the potion her mother had made for her. She knew that just a handful of moments ago she'd remembered the taste…

Now, there was nothing. Nothing but a tiny blank spot, about the size of a handful of glittering sparkles.

So *this* was how they died. Memories sucked away, one sparkle at a time, until nothing was left but a shell.

Yes, sighed the ocean. *Yes, give them all to us.*

Lucy sighed, a deep sound of resignation. Too good to be true, she supposed, after all. But at least she'd bought Edgar some time.

The fox nipped her ear.

Whether the two were causally link or whether it was mere coincidence, with the fox's nip suddenly sprang to mind the old children's rhyme, the one she'd deliberately avoiding thinking of since that day in the woods with Edgar.

Pay no heed to the bones of the sea.

Lucy narrowed her eyes.

There was another part to the song, one that not many people remembered. But Mama had remembered, and so Lucy remembered. The other part of the song, that lost, forgotten part, went like this:

Thrice for thee
and thrice for me
and thrice again
for the bones of the sea.

And another part, one she'd entirely forgotten hearing until just now, one she could hear as though Granny was there speaking it to her—she knew it was Granny's voice, even though Granny had never lived long enough to speak to her.

Price of the sea
paid thrice for thee,
keep my memories
safe for me.

"Fox," she said carefully. "What does it mean to pay no heed to the bones of the sea?"

Ignore them, the fox said simply. *They lie.*

"And you?" she said. "You are what, bones of the meadow?"

The fox licked her ear.

Bones of the meadow, faithful be.

Lucy narrowed her eyes at the orcas. "I think," she said carefully, "that I would like to go home now."

For a moment, everything stilled, a great in-taking of breath that could have been the precursor to a sigh or a storm—and for a second, Lucy couldn't predict which it would be.

Then, suddenly, the orcas swept below her and twisted, one balancing her its nose as it hurtled toward the sky.

Lucy flailed, caught her balance—such as it was—and threw her head back. Laughing seemed too trivial for such a wild rush, but she grinned fiercely, clutching at the little fox as the water around grew lighter and lighter—both in colour and in weight.

They broke through the surface of the sea with a splash like a tsunami, and Lucy shouted, half joy, and half defiance.

The whale rushed her through the water, dark as liquid night, the cove ahead only a thin, pale crescent below the stars.

But soon enough, it was close enough to see properly, even in the dim lighting—was it that dim? Surely the beach shouldn't be lit up like that, not (Lucy glanced upward) with the sky now velvet black.

And yet, there, in front of her, she could see the beach as though all the sand was glowing. And on the beach, Edgar sat, face drawn tight with worry and sorrow—until he spotted her, gliding in to shore in the dark, riding a whale that glowed like bones in the moonlight, accompanied by a fox much the same.

He leapt to his feet, splashing to the water's edge, in to his ankles, his knees, wading toward her.

And Lucy slid from the back of the orca when the water grew too shallow for it to come any farther, and she waded in to meet him, and she wasn't entirely sure whether it was she who swept him up into a fierce embrace, the soft and bony fox cradled between them like a promise of things to come, or whether it was he who initiated the hug. Either way, as though they'd held a rational discussion and mutually agreed upon it, they held each other's hands as they waded up to the shore.

They made the shallows, and then the beach, and Lucy's footsteps scrunched in the sand—sand which, she realised with a start, was not sand at all. It was bone, millions of tiny fragments of it, and in the dark it glowed just as the whales and the fox had, just like glowing ember fungus or phosphorescence, blue and gold, a whole beach of it, and as she watched the glow turned to a glimmer which caused the air to shimmer, and the entirety of it seemed awake, alive, aware.

Apparitions faded in and out of view, often golden, sometimes sapphire or magenta, glimmering, shimmering, barely there.

Instinctively, Lucy bent—first to let the fox down to the ground, and then to scoop up a handful of the strange phosphorescence of the beach.

Electric shivers shot through her.

As she cupped the bone fragments there in her hand—cold and heavy like an anchor in the night— she could feel them whispering.

Lucy raised them to her ear, as though a little more volume was all she required to unlock the secrets of the universe.

Alack, the whispers continued just as undecipherable—but the bone fox rubbed against her ankles.

"What *is* it?" Edgar whispered.

Lucy crouched. "A friend." She stroked the fox's bony ears. "Why are the bones awake now, little fox? What has changed?"

The ocean's taint, came the answer. *You have cleared the ocean's tainted claim from all the bones.*

Lucy blinked.

But true enough, Edgar was walking and talking, no longer catatonic like he had been.

"How?" was all she managed.

Nine memories were required, said the fox, *and nine you paid. The others who came to the sea came in despair, came hopeless. But you...*

Images swirled around her, flapping and flittering like a swarm of over-large butterflies, people walking, spacey-eyed and blank, to the water's edge; she felt disgust sour her stomach as the ocean dragged the people in and spat them out, and the disgust was the ocean's in that moment when it realised that its prey held not the memories that it sought.

Longing filled her, so deep that cold tears spilled down her cheeks and she gasped. Home. She just wanted home. But home was long gone, far away, left behind on a planet impossibly distant in a galaxy impossibly large, carried here oh, so far away on the back of a comet streaming through space, and all the water wanted was its home.

Lucy choked out a sob. "But why here?" she fumbled through the sadness. The ocean elsewhere didn't remember like this, didn't yearn.

Happenstance, the fox replied. *Sometimes that is all there is to it.*

Edgar smoothed the tears away from Lucy's cheeks, crouching so he could wrap himself around her. "What's wrong?" he said, face lit oddly by the blue and gold and pink of the glowing bones. "What is it?"

Lucy shook her head. Nothing. Nothing was wrong. "The curse has lifted," she said, and even as she did she realised that something more than memories was missing from her mind. The curse had exerted a kind of persistent pressure she hadn't even known was there, until now… it was gone.

Edgar's eyes widened. He pressed his fingertips to his cheekbone. Then the wonder fell from his eyes and he stared at her, sombre. "What did you do?"

Lucy shrugged. "Thrice for thee and thrice for me," she said, and laughed when his face grew horrified. "Memories," she explained. "The ocean wanted memories of home. Still wants memories," she added, glancing back out at the dark expanse beside them, the silver trail of the moon wider now. She could feel it there, lingering beyond the salty spray, the seaweed taste: that longing, that yearning for home. She would have to feed it regularly, she suspected.

Sure enough, a breath of Mist was already forming nearby, over the surface of the waves that were growing gradually more insistent.

Cautiously, Lucy felt around the tiny, sparkle-sized holes in her memories. It seemed like such an absurdly small price to pay, really. After all, she there were always new memories to be made.

Lucy pursed her lips, stared at Edgar for one long, charged moment.

"What?" His voice sounded cautious, hesitant.

Lucy smiled. Stood, dragging him with her. Tucked herself under his arm so she could lean against his warm chest, and he against the top of her head. Then she led him slowly down the beach, while bones whispered and the beach glimmered gold and blue and pink with every footstep as Lucy eyed the embankment for a lower place to climb.

There were always new memories to be made of home, and from what she understood, the making of could be rather pleasant.

**Price of the sea
paid thrice for thee,
keep my memories
safe for me.**

Twenty years ago, Lucy could never have predicted that her life would turn out like this. The western beach, its golden sand still mingled with a large helping of dull white bone fragments, seemed to glow in the evening light as the sun sank to the sea.

A shriek drew Lucy's gaze a few hundred paces to her right, nearly at the end of the cove, where six-year-old Bessie splashed furiously at her older brother. Behind the both, barely visible in the bright light of the setting sun, a fox darted and yapped, translucent as though made only of light and bone.

Lucy smiled, lips cracking a little under their film of salt. She licked it away.

"Ready?" Edgar asked from behind, reaching down to smooth Lucy's hair from her face.

She leaned into his caress. "Nearly."

To her left, sprawled out on the red picnic rug, Mama snorted. "You'd live here if he let you, I think."

Lucy smiled again, not bothering to argue. Besides. She wasn't sure her mother wasn't right.

Others had fallen in love with the bones of the meadow; the creatures and livestock that passed away there had their bones left as offerings to the sky, and once the carcasses had returned almost fully to the earth, the bones were gathered up and incorporated into household objects; objects which never broke, or got lost, or misplaced. Objects as faithful as the bones from which they were made.

Still others had come to prefer the forest, with bones that could be carefully carved into protective amulets and healing wards; and some had even ventured up beyond the mountains to the deserts, and had found there a sparse scattering of tiny bones, mice and snakes and lizards mostly, who told the truth—and only the truth.

But Lucy? Lucy had fallen first for the bones of the sea, and over time their tall tales had sounded less like lies and more like stories: stories she could lose herself in, could sink luxuriantly into, feeling them close around her like the warmth of waves.

So it was here she brought her children most often, here to the shush and hush of the tides, here to the taste of salt spray on lips and the mineral smell of sand that was always either a little too hot or else a little too cold; here, where the sun sank and stars appeared like diamonds lighting up the sky, a swathe of sparkles like memories.

"Come on," Edgar said. "If we leave now, we can take our time in the woods."

Mama sat upright at that. "Ember fungus," she muttered.

Lucy laughed. It was the easiest thing in the world to bring Mama; always she needed something fancy for her potions, made even stronger now with the knowledge the bones had shared with her. Even Granny's old journals had begun to make sense when they were read beneath old King Jack by the light of a pair of gently illuminated antlers.

And the Mist?

Lucy called to her children down the beach, watched with smiling heart as they gave one last tremendous splash then made their way back to their family, gathered up the blanket and shook it free of sand and bone alike.

She bent to caress the fox that wound around her ankles.

As they climbed up the steps now carved into the embankment, the ocean sent tendrils of its Mist to farewell them.

Feed meeeee… it sighed.

Lips quirking, Lucy flicked her fingers at the gentle Mist. A sparkle, so tiny, flew from her to it. A tiny memory, naught but two seconds of smiles with the taste of salt and a warm breeze on her cheeks while her hair flew free and her heart filled high.

The Mist shrank back, satisfied.

Lucy hefted Bessie up the last step, her small, bony body warm and full of life.

Due to a peculiar combination of luck, Mama's willingness to take a chance on a potion in Granny's journals, and Lucy's own instincts, her daughter could see the Mist any given day she liked.

And if the price Lucy had to pay for that was a few tiny memories of home offered every so often—for the sake of *her* home, for the sake of her family—well then. They were a renewable resource, at least to an extent.

"Mummy," Bessie said, turning back to the ocean. "Why does it always tell me I can't go home?"

Lucy ruffled Bessie's dark hair and smiled. "The bones of the sea tell stories, Bessie. I've told you before. Pay them no heed."

The fox yipped and dashed on ahead. Bessie and her brother shrieked, following it into the forest.

Lucy turned for a last look over her shoulder, and smiled at the ocean as it surged against the shore, a literal wave goodbye. "Keep them safe for me," she murmured to it with a farewell nod.

Edgar squeezed her hand.

She squeezed his back.

And, hand in hand as though they'd been together so long it wasn't a thing that needed discussing any more, they headed back to the woods.

A FOX OF STORMS AND STARLIGHT

CHAPTER ONE

SIX YEARS AGO, I SAVED a fox in the bush. It was only because my dog died. At the time, it felt like a pretty crappy bargain.

It was the first day of autumn—not by the calendar, but by the fresh bite in the morning air, the golden quality of the light as it lit the main road through town in the mid-afternoon.

Sailor was a big, black shaggy thing, something like a Newfoundland, a lively shadow in the golden light, and I was eleven.

I'm sorry to be starting any story this way, but the fact of the matter is, this where it all began.

I'll spare you the awful details. Enough to say that Sailor had got out of the yard somehow, and had been hit by a small-ish truck careening down the highway that split our tiny town in two as it blatantly ignored the speed limit.

I saw it happen.

And although I cradled him in my lap as the smell of burnt-out brakes and hot asphalt and turning leaves filled the air, his giant, furry black head all of him I could hold, there was nothing I could do.

There was nothing anyone could do.

I knew that, but it didn't stop the knot of frustration and guilt in my chest, or the taste of bile in the back of my throat every time I closed my eyes and saw the truck hitting him, again and again and again.

It took years for that vision to fade.

But that evening, only a few hours after it had happened, everything still felt fresh, and raw.

Sunny, my sister, was only nine at the time. She cried for hours, just sobbing like she'd never breathe right again.

I'd cried a little, at the scene with Sailor's head lying in my lap as one, brown eye stared up at nothing.

It had been mercifully fast, there was that.

And the driver had copped a massive fine—speeding, reckless driving, I think they even defected his truck—and came to visit us later, a big, potbellied man standing on our front verandah, shuffling his royal blue cap round and round and round in his hands as he apologised.

But that evening, with Sunny sobbing her heart out on the couch in the living room and Mum and Dad trying desperately to console her as dinner burned on the stove, I couldn't cry, even though the acrid scent of burning soy sauce, scorching brown sugar and smoking rice wine from the marinade prickled the back of my throat and the corners of my eyes.

I was the eldest, and I had to be responsible.

Possibly, if I'd been just a little more responsible, Sailor wouldn't have died.

So I slipped out the glass slider from the family room to the deck while Sunny cried, glancing up at the two storeys of our moody grey house behind me before jumping down from the rail-less deck to the lawn, and set out for the gate in the back fence.

I couldn't cry, and I didn't want to add anything to an already chaotic and stressful situation inside—but I couldn't stay there, either.

In the gaps between the gum trees to the west, the sky tinged to red and gold at the horizon, the sun sinking slowly into oblivion. I'm pretty sure I didn't know the word oblivion back then, but I knew what it meant, how it felt—and I craved it, desperately.

Anything would be better than the gaping hole in my chest.

And so, because I didn't know where to find it or how to get there, I stalked through the bush, pushing myself until I breathed hard and my lungs ached and sweat ringed me, chasing the way that hard exercise elevated me over my constantly looping thoughts.

Directly above, dark, heavy clouds obscured the sky, and the air was thick, heavy, humid.

Beneath the smell of dry gum leaves and even drier dirt, I could catch a hint of ozone, and occasionally the wind turned cool for a breath as it gusted against my skin, promising a late-evening storm.

I strode harder, faster, outpacing the video looping in my mind of the truck's impact.

When the first drops of rain spat at me from out of the sky, I barely noticed. My skin was filmed with sweat, slick and salty, and the peppering of rainwater barely added to it.

That was at first.

But within minutes, it became clear that those first pattering spits had been the early foreshadowing of a storm darker and more intense than any I remembered.

Thunder rolled across the sky, distant and grumbling at first, a lazy background chorus to the rhythmic melody of the rain as it splattered down on grey-green leaves and red-tinged twigs, turning the silvered bark of an old, dead gum to deep grey and making the spiky, tussocky grass seem oddly luminescent in the dying light.

I stood under a grey gum with stains down its trunk that the rain was turning orange, arms wrapped around myself, shivering hard—and for the briefest instant, thought about not going home.

Mum and Dad would pitch a fit.

And I had to be responsible.

I turned, dark t-shirt plastered to my skin, dark hair sticking to my face and clinging to my neck and began trudging my way back.

The storm closed over properly, clouds rolling over the horizon and cutting off the thin scythe of blood-coloured sunset, making the bush dark and unwelcoming in the premature night.

Lightning flashed.

Thunder cracked hot on its heels.

I jumped—and stared hard at the gap between two ghost-barked trees, where for a second, I was sure I'd seen a pair of eyes.

Nothing moved.

Nothing except the drenching rain, anyway, weighing down the branches that tossed fitfully in the wind.

My pulse slowly calmed.

There were rumours we'd all grown up with here in Jilamatang that spoke of something strange and dark... But that was in the forest north of here, in the pines, the plantation—not here, not in the natural, native bush.

I shivered.

The smell of wet dirt and soaked bark rose around me, undercut by eucalypt and ozone.

If anything had the power to wash away the hurt inside me, this storm was it. I tipped my face to the sky, imagining that the rain washing over me had the ability to wash me inside as well, and the raindrops splattered hard on my cheekbones, my chin, my tightly closed eyelids.

More lightning.

More thunder, cracking over the constant hiss of the falling rain.

And in the distance, something eerie, lifting the hairs on the back of my neck: a strange kind of high-pitched yowl, a cry that rang with moonlight and distance, cutting straight through the noise of the storm.

Bolts of lightning streaked across the sky—one—two—three in the space of half a second, followed immediately by a growling crack of thunder so immense it vibrated in my chest.

I ducked down instinctively into a crouch.

There, in the corner of my eye…

I froze with my arms over my head.

The strange cries came again—and they were closer. I stared hard at the place, low to the ground, where I was sure I'd seen something small, maybe the size of a cat.

Flash. Growl.

Rain spitting down.

There. Right there. A small animal, pointy ears, light coloured chin and throat…

The strange, eerie cries came a third time, and my heart pounded fiercely. Whatever was making the noise, it was close. Really close.

The little creature across from me reacted too, flattening itself to the ground.

My jaw twitched.

My heart pounded.

My fingertips bit into my upper arms.

Stay? Go?

Run? Freeze?

The hairs on my neck prickled again and goose-bumps broke out all over me.

Cold dread formed a knot in my stomach.

Something was coming.

Something worse than the storm.

I had to get home.

I made it halfway to standing—and a series of strange, awful noises made me freeze again. They were sharp, clacking, squealing sounds, like someone knocking two echoing stones against each other, interspersed with high-pitched yowling...

And the creature in the darkness screamed.

I threw my back against the gumtree behind me, pressing hard against it.

My heart hammered.

I peered back and forth in the dark, eyes wide.

Rain drenched down, but my throat was dry.

My pulse pounded faster.

The little creature screamed again—and as lightning flashed, I saw it on its back, legs slashing wildly at the air as something attacked.

The awful, clacking-yowling noises sounded right in front of me.

I slapped my hands over my ears, gasping. Water ran down my face, into my mouth, my eyes.

It was hurting.

Whatever the small thing was, it was getting hurt, and I'd seen enough animals hurting today.

Something in my chest snapped.

I flung myself across the ground, leaping tussocks and a fallen branch before I crashed to my knees.

I crawled closer, desperate, gasping for oxygen through the heavy curtains of rain.

I couldn't see it. Where?

Somewhere here, near the base of that tree...

The yowling screeched right next to my ear. I cowered against the ground, spiky grass pricking my face, wet-earth smell smothering me—but now, there was a strange mustiness too, a cousin to wet-dog smell.

At the next flash of lightning, I saw it.

The creature was a fox—and something barely visible was attacking it, only the gleam of eye or flicker of teeth visible in the gloom.

But the damage was real enough.

The little fox's side had been opened right up, and in the bright, stark flashes of heavenly electricity, the blood was dark, thinned by the constant rain.

No.

No more animals were going to die today.

Not when this time, I could do something about it.

I snatched at a branch on the ground that turned out to be more of a glorified twig, and launched myself toward the creature.

I had no idea what was attacking it, but I screamed and waved my handful of twiggy leaves anyway, batting them in the air like I knew what I was doing.

The horrible clacking cries ceased abruptly.

With one long, low rumble, the rain began to ebb.

I poised, waiting.

But nothing came.

The attackers were gone.

Still gasping for air, pulse galloping in my throat, I sat next to the fox and shifted it carefully into my lap, realising as I tasted salt that I was crying.

I huddled over, trying to shelter the poor creature from the slackening rain, running my fingers over its wiry cheek—over and over and over and over.

"Please," I sobbed, throat tight and aching, chest constricted. "Please. Please don't die. Please."

Please, I prayed to anything that might be listening. *No more death. Not today.*

Not today.

Another gust of cool air washed over the clearing, taking the last of the rain with it—and lifting the goosebumps on my arms again.

And as it did, I could have sworn I heard a voice. *Neither do I wish him to die now.*

I shivered, drawing the fox close, like it was a stuffed animal I could hug for comfort—its comfort or mine, I couldn't say. I glanced around the dripping bush, eyes wide. The rumours spoke of an evil presence, and I could easily believe that might be what had attacked the fox.

But a voice? No one had ever mentioned a voice.

There was nothing to be seen, and anyway the voice had sounded kindly—and didn't want the fox to die.

Assuming I hadn't just imagined it, of course. Which, half-drowned by grief, the other half drowned by the storm... An over-active imagination seemed highly likely.

Can you fix him? I thought it hard, though, just in case someone really was listening.

Something shifted in my lap.

Around us, the world stilled, dazed from the storm, but also something more, something watching, something waiting, as the bush held its collective breath.

The only sound was the occasional drip of rainwater from the gum leaves onto a fallen log—no insects, no wind, no rustling of leaves.

Just... stillness.

And the fox, who shivered in my lap.

The clouds tore open, revealing a ragged triangle of stars that glittered in the fox's eye as it blinked open and stared up at me.

My chest snagged.

My throat ached from crying, and a headache was forming in the back of my head.

But the fox blinked up at me—alive.

I ran a finger down it again, from nose to cheek to ear to shoulder, all the way down its side to its thick, bushy tail—and the wound in its side began to close.

Laboriously, it hauled itself to its front legs.

I tried to stop it—"No, it's okay, you can stay here, I'll look after you"—but it lifted its top lip to show half-hearted teeth, and staggered away.

As it did, I thought perhaps its fur began to shrink.

And suddenly, it looked larger in the night—as large as a dog, as large as Sailor…

But I blinked, and it was just a trick of the light, because the creature that darted away into the bushes like nothing was wrong at all was clearly a fox, the size of a large cat or maybe a small beagle, and nothing more.

And if something screamed in the night not long afterward, and the cry sounded horribly, horribly human?

Well.

I was halfway back toward home again by then, and I pressed my fingertips to my lower eyelids and prayed my parents wouldn't murder me for getting home so late.

Keep reading! Head to
www.inkprintpress.com/amylaurens/
stormfoxes/
to buy your copy now!

ABOUT THE AUTHOR

AMY LAURENS is an Australian author of fantasy and science fiction for both adults and young adults. She also writes non-fiction books, often on various aspects of writing. Also dogs. Lots of dogs.

After completing a university education involving many twists and turns—through more faculties than ought reasonably to exist—Amy now spends her day as a high-school English teacher. No, she is not going to do your homework for you. Not even the English bit. Sorry. Have a cookie instead.

Amy has written the award-winning *Sanctuary* series about Edge, a 13-year-old girl who discovers that the land of the fairies is in trouble; *How Not To Acquire A Castle*, a humorous fantasy novel that follows Mercury's attempts to graduate at the top of the Evil Overlord class and acquire herself a castle; the *Storm Foxes* series about love and magic and family and depression in small-town Australia; and more.

You can find her at www.AmyLaurens.com.